THE DANGEROUS DIAMOND

Look for these books in the
Clue™ series:

Clue™

THE DANGEROUS DIAMOND

Book created by A. E. Parker

Written by Marie Jacks

Based on characters from the Parker Brothers® game

A Creative Media Applications Production

SCHOLASTIC INC.
New York Toronto London Auckland Sydney

Special thanks to: Susan Nash, Laura Millhollin, Maureen Taxter, Jean Feiwel, Ellie Berger, Greg Holch, Dona Smith, Nancy Smith, John Simko, David Tommasino, Jennifer Presant, and Elizabeth Parisi

ISBN 0-590-62377-X

12 11 10 9 8 7 6 5 4 3 2 1   6 7 8 9/9 0 1/0

Printed in the U.S.A.   40

First Scholastic printing, September 1996

Contents

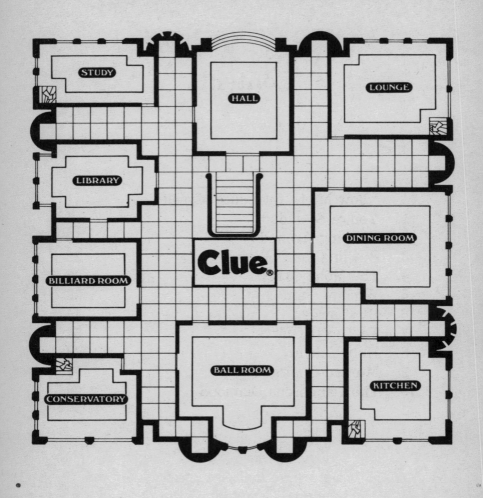

Allow Me to Introduce Myself . . .

G**REETINGS!**

I am Reginald Boddy, your host for another visit to my wonderful mansion.

Over the years, there have been many exciting times here. Visitors come and go and, on more occasions than I care to remember, my valuables have gone with them. Sometimes stealing isn't enough and my visitors turn to murder, as well.

Let's take the wraps off what happened last time at the mansion. The episode involved a mummy and a missing ancient treasure — or so my guests thought. My maid, Mrs. White, strangled me because I was dressed up like the mummy. I'd be just as dead as one if the Rope hadn't gotten tangled up in the mummy sheets.

In a few moments I shall be joining Mrs. White and my guests in the Library. Yes, against all common sense I've invited them back for another visit. I do like how they fill up the place — when they're not filling up their pockets with my things.

Since you're no doubt brave and brilliant, would you please help me keep track of them?

There are six suspects, including my maid, Mrs. White. (I will never be a suspect in any wrongdoing. You have my word on this, as a gentleman.) The six you need to keep track of are:

Mr. Green: Find a dictionary and look up the word *greed*. It wouldn't surprise me if you find a picture of Mr. Green in place of the definition.

Colonel Mustard: Ever since he was once called yellow as a boy, he's taken to dueling to settle any dispute. Once he was arrested for jaywalking and offered to settle the matter with the traffic officer by using pistols at dawn.

Mrs. Peacock: She believes only the most proper people deserve a seat at her table. Being so particular, Mrs. Peacock often dines alone.

Professor Plum: A highly educated chap who would be happy to read you a list of his many honorary degrees. That is, once he remembers where he left his reading glasses.

Miss Scarlet: If it's true that diamonds are a girl's best friend, then Miss Scarlet isn't one to share her friends with anyone. She is an attractive woman — attracted to diamonds, rubies, gold, and silver.

Mrs. White: She is amazing at keeping the mansion clean. More amazing is how she cleaned out its safe without my catching her.

*   *   *

There. A more stunning collection of guests you won't find anywhere. Make certain that they don't stun you with their criminal antics.

Please know that at the end of each chapter, a list of rooms, suspects, and weapons will be provided so that you may keep track of events at the mansion.

Well, so much for the overture. It's time for the real music to begin.

The curtain on our first adventure is about to rise in the Library.

1.
You're So Jaded

"I'M SORRY I AM LATE," MR. BODDY TOLD his guests as he entered the room. "Silly me. I'd forgotten where I'd asked you to meet me. By mistake, I took the *secret* secret passage from the Conservatory to the Lounge, when I remembered I was meeting you here in the Library. Please forgive my tardiness."

"You're forgiven," said Mrs. Peacock, "provided you have something worthwhile to show us."

"As you wish," Mr. Boddy said, proceeding to show a recent acquisition to his guests.

"I've never seen anything quite like it . . . I think," said Professor Plum.

"It's lovely," said Mrs. White, admiring the small treasure. "It should belong to a woman who will appreciate its uniqueness — like me."

"It must be worth a fortune," said Mr. Green.

"It's precious and goes perfectly with what I'm wearing," added Miss Scarlet.

"It's perfect in every detail," said Professor Plum.

"Men would kill to get their hands on it," said Colonel Mustard.

"It's exquisite," said Mrs. Peacock.

What the guests were admiring was a life-size sparrow carved from jade.

Professor Plum leaned forward and examined the jade carving with an eagle eye. "It's perfect in every detail," he concluded.

"You already said that," said Miss Scarlet.

"He's such a birdbrain," whispered Mr. Green.

"And a loon," added Mrs. Peacock.

"Where did you get this fine-feathered friend?" asked Miss Scarlet, craning for a closer look.

"I found it in a gallery near the shore," said Mr. Boddy. "It didn't come chirp — I mean, cheap," he added.

"The owner sounds cuckoo," said Mrs. White.

"I hope you didn't get rooked," said Mr. Green.

Mr. Boddy chuckled. "You may think that I'm gull-ible, but you're wrong. Let's just say the piece of jade is worth a million dollars on the gem market. The beautiful carving at least doubles its value."

"Is it really worth two million dollars?" asked Professor Plum, swallowing hard. "That's not chicken feed."

"It's worth two million dollars," Mr. Boddy assured his guests.

"Did you buy it as a lark?" asked Colonel Mustard.

5

"No, it's always been a sparrow," said Mr. Boddy.

"The sparrow is certainly no turkey," said Miss Scarlet. "I wish I had that bird in my hand."

"Mr. Boddy, you should give it to me," insisted Mrs. Peacock. "After all, I'm named after a bird."

"Which? An old coot?" joked Miss Scarlet.

"How rude!" snapped Mrs. Peacock.

"Give me the sparrow and I'll be your lovebird forever," cooed Miss Scarlet.

"Before my grandfather shortened the family name, it was actually Bobwhite," said Mrs. White. "So I should get the bird."

"You sound like a bunch of vultures," said Mr. Boddy.

Mr. Green cautiously glanced around at the Library shelves. He spotted the Candlestick high on a shelf and decided to use the weapon in an attempt to snatch the sparrow.

"Let's talk turkey," said Colonel Mustard. "That bird would make a mighty nice nest egg. How about carving it up so each of us can take a piece home?"

"Oh, it wouldn't be worth its weight in birdseed if I did that," explained Mr. Boddy.

"Mr. Boddy, why do you insist on keeping your possessions to yourself?" asked an angry Colonel Mustard. "It's not fair!"

"Now, Colonel, you'd better not ruffle my feathers further or I'll have to ask you to take wing and leave."

"Mr. Boddy is very upset," whispered Miss Scarlet to Mrs. White. "We'd best walk on eggshells around him tonight."

In her mind, Mrs. White envisioned the Wrench — right where she had left it in the Conservatory.

"I hope you're taking good care of that jade specimen," said Mrs. Peacock. "It would be horrible if someone stole it."

"Truly," said Mr. Boddy. "And which particular 'someone' do you have in mind?"

Mrs. Peacock thought about the Revolver she had hidden in the Ball Room. "None of us, surely," she told Mr. Boddy.

Professor Plum yawned. "Well, I don't know about the rest of you, but I'm ready to curl up in my little nest for a good night's sleep."

"Me too," added Mr. Green. "You know what they say, 'The early bird catches the worm.'"

"I can't wait to get under my goose-down comforter," said Mrs. Peacock.

" 'Birds of a feather flock together,' " sang Miss Scarlet as she, too, headed up the stairs for bed.

"Good night," said Colonel Mustard. "Or should I say, 'Tweet, tweet'?"

"I'll just grab my feather duster and I'll be out of here, too," said Mrs. White, closing the door behind her.

7

"Alone at last," sighed Mr. Boddy, admiring his treasure.

Several minutes later . . .

Several minutes later, Mr. Boddy exited the Library with the jade sparrow in hand.

He stopped to make certain that the mansion's timepieces were in sync.

"Hmmm, the grandfather clock is slowing down," he observed. "Better keep up, Grandpa, or you'll lose your place of honor in the Hall."

After resetting the clock to the current time, Mr. Boddy proceeded to the Lounge. He had to place a phone call about selling the jade sparrow. But before he could finish dialing, he was attacked by a guest with the Wrench and was knocked out.

At the same time, another guest was leaving the Ball Room. She carried the Revolver.

Mr. Boddy's original attacker took the jade carving, but before leaving the room she was attacked by a guest with the Knife.

"Any way you slice it," the guest taunted, "the jade bird is mine." But before the guest could make off with the sparrow, she was attacked by a guest with the Lead Pipe.

The guest with the Lead Pipe grabbed the sparrow and fled the Lounge through the *secret* secret passage connecting that room to another room, which was dark.

8

For a moment, in the darkness, the thief forgot where he was.

"Let's see," he whispered. "Did I go from the Conservatory to the Lounge or from the Lounge to the Conservatory?"

He didn't hear someone come up behind him.

"Professor, perhaps this will clear out your mental cobwebs," said the guest with the Wrench, who had recovered from a previous attack.

"Can't we discuss this like two civilized beings?" he asked.

"No," she replied, whacking the professor over the head.

She took the valuable jade and ran to the Dining Room and then into the Kitchen.

Just as she got there, she was confronted by the guest coming from the Ball Room.

"Give me the jade," the guest said, "or I'll shoot."

"Why don't you fly away?" asked the guest with the jade.

They struggled and the gun went off.

A bullet grazed the shoulder of the guest with the Wrench.

"Oh, I'm wounded!" she cried, handing over the sparrow.

The guest with the Revolver took the sparrow into the Billiard Room and was attacked with the Candlestick. Stunned, the guest lost the jade sparrow to the attacker.

9

"Pardon me while I fly the coop," the attacker said, going with the sparrow into the Hall.

Another guest waited there. "I hope you're not planning to take wing with that bird," said the guest, attacking with the remaining weapon.

The sparrow changed hands.

And the guest now possessing the sparrow fled into the remaining room.

WHO WAS LAST TO STEAL THE JADE SPARROW?

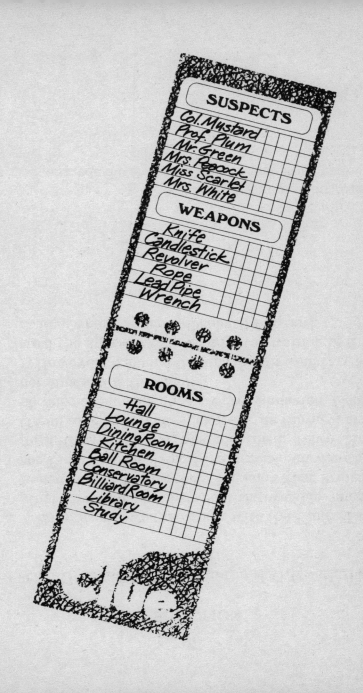

SOLUTION

COLONEL MUSTARD in the HALL with the ROPE

Miss Scarlet was the guest with the Knife. The other two female guests had the weapons mentioned earlier in the story. We know that Professor Plum had the Lead Pipe because he was the forgetful guest who was identified. Since Mr. Green took the Candlestick from the Library, and because the female guests were eliminated, Colonel Mustard is the thief.

However, knowing that his guests would try to steal the sparrow, Mr. Boddy was waiting in the Study, where he netted Colonel Mustard.

2.
Fiddling Around

MR. BODDY CALLED HIS GUESTS INTO the Conservatory.

While the guests looked on, Mr. Boddy pulled out a strangely shaped case and began to open it.

"That thing looks like the cases the old gangsters used to carry submachine guns in," said an alarmed Professor Plum.

"I hope it's not a submachine gun or we're sunk," moaned Mrs. White.

"No, it's nothing of the kind," Mr. Boddy assured his guests. "In fact, it's one of the greatest creations of Western civilization."

"You have my high school graduation picture?" asked Miss Scarlet.

Shaking his head no, Mr. Boddy showed the guests a beautiful, old violin.

"Something new for your musical instrument collection?" asked Mrs. Peacock.

"Actually, I plan on playing this one," said Mr. Boddy.

"I used to play drums when I was younger," said Mr. Green. He took the Lead Pipe from his tweed jacket pocket and banged it against the floor. "See?"

" 'See'? Don't you mean, 'Hear'?" joked Mrs. White.

"I can see and hear why you gave up the drums," observed Mrs. Peacock, covering her ears.

"Mr. Boddy, I didn't know that you played music," said Colonel Mustard.

"I'm just starting," said Mr. Boddy. "So I thought I'd buy myself a decent instrument."

Professor Plum took a step forward, peered over his glasses and gave the violin a thorough inspection. "It looks like a good fiddle," he concluded.

"It isn't a fiddle," said Mr. Boddy. "It's a violin."

"What's the difference?" asked Mrs. White.

"A fiddle can be bought for a song," explained Mr. Boddy. "But a violin is much more expensive. Mine, for instance, is a Stradivarius."

"Stradivarius?" asked Mr. Green. "Isn't that a type of pasta, like rigatoni or fettuccine?"

"Stradivari was the most famous Italian violin maker. His violins are hundreds of years old and are among the finest in the world," explained Mr. Boddy. "This one is worth nearly a million dollars!"

"A million dollars?" said Mr. Green. "That sum is like music to my ears."

14

"I'm absolutely mad about that Strad," said Miss Scarlet. She reached in her purse, where she had the Rope. "I can't wait to get my string on those strings," she said to herself.

"I'd be glad to have the Strad, and sad if I can't," whispered Mrs. Peacock.

"It's a very fine instrument, no doubt. But, Mr. Boddy, do you know anything about playing the violin?" asked Mrs. White.

"Well, I know that unlike the guitar, the violin has no frets," said Mr. Boddy.

"Oh, good, we wouldn't want you to fret," joked Miss Scarlet.

"The front of the violin is called the belly," Mr. Boddy added.

"When he plays, it'll sound like a belly flop," whispered Professor Plum. Planning to steal the priceless violin himself, Professor Plum checked his pocket for the Revolver.

Mr. Boddy pointed to the thin part of the violin. "This part is called the neck."

Colonel Mustard put a hand into his hunting jacket pocket, to check for the weapon concealed there. "I can easily adjust the Wrench to fit around that neck," he murmured.

Mr. Boddy next pointed to a small piece of wood over which the strings were stretched. "This is called the bridge. You move the bow back and forth near it to produce the sound by vibrating the strings," he explained.

"So you'll cross that bridge when you come to it?" asked Professor Plum.

Mr. Boddy demonstrated. Unfortunately, the sound he produced more closely resembled a screeching cat than music.

Miss Scarlet covered her ears. "Turn it off," she pleaded. "I'll do anything, just stop that noise!"

"So I need a little practice," admitted Mr. Boddy.

"A little?" mocked Mrs. Peacock. "You're lucky we didn't have you arrested for disturbing the peace."

"I'll get better with lessons," promised Mr. Boddy.

"What are the strings made of?" asked Mr. Green.

"Catgut," said Mr. Boddy.

"Guts?" whispered Mrs. Peacock. "How rude!" Furious that Mr. Boddy would own such an impolite instrument, she checked her purse for the Knife hidden there.

"Actually, I found Mr. Boddy's playing to my liking," said Mrs. White.

"Are you hoping for a raise in pay?" asked Miss Scarlet.

"Play us a few more notes," said Mrs. White.

Happy to oblige, Mr. Boddy tried to, but his technique was awful. The violin made more horrible screeching noises.

"Good. That should scare any mice away," said Mrs. White.

The demonstration over, Mr. Boddy asked his guests to depart. They last saw him carefully putting the instrument back in its case and turning off the lights.

Several hours later . . .

Several hours later, a female guest, who had not had a weapon earlier, entered the darkened Conservatory. Using the Candlestick for light, she crept toward the violin case.

"Selling the Strad will pad my bank account," she said. "With it I can pay for a rad pad in Trinidad."

But before she could steal the instrument, she was hit over the head by another guest wielding the Wrench.

"I play the Wrench better than Mr. Boddy plays his fiddle," said the second guest. Stepping over the fallen guest and the Candlestick, the guest with the Wrench picked up the instrument case. "Here, little Straddy," he whispered, "come to daddy."

He fled the room and went into the Lounge.

But there, much to his astonishment, he found a female guest jumping Rope.

"What *are* you doing?" he asked.

"Staying fit as a fiddle," she said.

"You're quite good with that Rope," the first guest observed.

"You want to see one of my famous Rope tricks?" the second guest asked. Before he could respond, she tied him up.

"Very good," he said. "Now untie me."

"Sorry, no."

She stole the Stradivarius and raced out of the room. "I need to come up with a hiding place and quick," she told herself as she ran into the room with the shortest name.

There she was attacked by the guest with the Lead Pipe — and lost the violin.

"I have an ironclad place to stash the Strad," the new thief said.

But the room where the guest planned to hide the instrument was occupied by a guest browsing the shelves for something to read.

"Looking for something in particular?" the thief asked, hiding the instrument case behind his back.

"Mr. Boddy's sudden interest in music has made me want to learn more," the browsing guest said. He took a book down from the shelf. "Ah, here's one about a singing dog called *The Hound of Music*. Have you read it?"

"No, but I heard it was a howler," the thief said.

"How about this one?" the second guest asked,

taking down another book. "It's called *For Whom the Bell Tolls*."

"Hmmm," said the thief. "It has a certain ring to it."

"Here's one about a violin-playing cow," the browsing guest said, taking down a third book. "It's called *The Ox-Bow Incident*."

Pretending to care, the thief reached for the book — and was attacked by the browsing guest.

The instrument case changed hands again.

The guest with the violin fled into the Kitchen, and was confronted by the remaining female guest.

"Be a good lad and hand over that doodad," she ordered.

"What are you talking about?" the guest with the violin asked.

"Quit being a cad! Give me the Strad or I'll go stark raving mad!" she warned, swinging her weapon.

"I believe you," the guest said, handing over the instrument case.

WHO STOLE THE STRAD LAST?

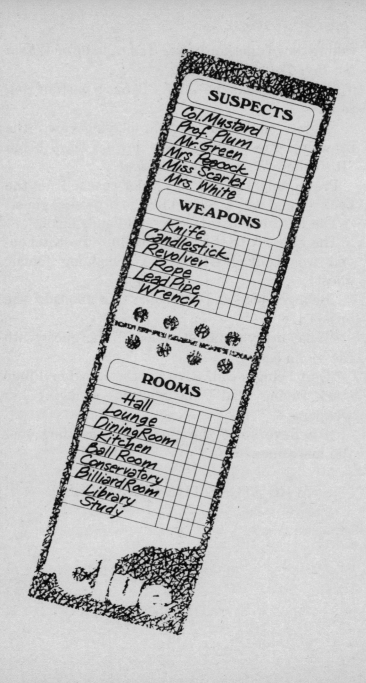

SOLUTION

MRS. PEACOCK

Since Mrs. White and Miss Scarlet were eliminated, the female thief must be Mrs. Peacock.

Unfortunately, when she opened the instrument case it was empty. Mr. Boddy had outsmarted her and hidden the violin elsewhere. To teach her a lesson, Mr. Boddy made her listen to him practicing the violin for hours.

3.
Bowling for Dollars

HEARING THAT MR. BODDY HAD A SPE-
cial gift for each of them, the guests waited eagerly in the Lounge.

"I'll bet he's giving me his pearl-handled Revolver," said Colonel Mustard. "It's the perfect
weapon for fighting a duel."

"I'm hoping for a jewel-encrusted tiara," said
Mrs. Peacock, "to wear at the next charity ball."

"I've had my eye on the stocks and bonds that
Mr. Boddy keeps in his safe," admitted Mr. Green.
"A man of my investment savvy could make a lot
of money with them."

"Mr. Boddy has a scientific drawing by Leo-
nardo da Vinci," said Professor Plum. "I'd love to
take it home and tape it over my bed."

"You're all wrong," predicted Miss Scarlet.
"The truth is that Mr. Boddy is in love with me
and wants me to have the enormous diamond en-
gagement ring that belonged to his mother."

"If Mr. Boddy wants to give me something
memorable, I'd be happy with a day off from cleaning," sighed Mrs. White.

At last Mr. Boddy entered, balancing six identical gift boxes, which he distributed.

The guests tore off the ribbons and wrapping paper, eager to discover what treasures lay in store.

"There must be some mistake," said a stunned Mrs. Peacock, pulling a short-sleeved and rather ugly shirt from her box. "This isn't my taste at all. I consider short-sleeved shirts to be most improper. A lady should never show off her arms in public. Worse yet, someone has stitched the inane name 'Birdie' on the front of this monstrous piece of apparel."

"I got a silly shirt, too," said a disappointed Colonel Mustard. "It has 'Hot Dog' stitched in yellow."

"If the shirt fits, wear it," joked Miss Scarlet.

"Mr. Boddy, is this your idea of a joke?" asked Colonel Mustard. "If so, I challenge you to a duel this very instant!"

"I like my shirt," said Miss Scarlet. She held up a white shirt with a cardinal red collar, bright ruby-colored buttons, and a bold crimson waistband. "It's so retro, like something out of the nineteen-fifties. But my nickname isn't 'Red,' which is stitched on the front."

"And I hate being called 'Greenie,' " said Mr. Green, holding up his shirt. "It rhymes with meanie."

" 'Peewee'?" asked Professor Plum, pointing to

the name stitched on the pocket of his own shirt. "I haven't been called that since I was a lad. Peewee Plum. Boy, that brings back memories I'd rather forget."

"Well, it's better than the name stitched on mine," said Mrs. White. " 'Mrs. Strike'? What kind of name is that? I may well go on strike if someone doesn't explain."

"Very well," said Mr. Boddy. "I thought a team sport would be a fun way to spend our afternoon together. So I had a bowling alley installed in the Hall and I ordered bowling shirts for each of you."

"A bowling alley in the Hall?" asked Mrs. White. "Something else for me to keep clean."

"Bowling?" asked Mrs. Peacock. "I think knocking down pins is rude."

"I hate bowling," said Colonel Mustard. "Have you ever tried dueling with bowling balls? They're much too heavy."

"Bowling is such a silly sport," sneered Mr. Green.

"As opposed to your favorite sport, tiddlywinks?" snapped Miss Scarlet.

"I'm sorry that you're not interested," said Mr. Boddy in a disappointed voice. "Because I was going to give twenty thousand dollars to each member of the winning team."

"There's nothing better than swinging an insanely heavy ball," said Miss Scarlet.

"Bowling is the second greatest game ever in-

24

vented," added Professor Plum. "After CLUE, of course."

"If the pins are knocked down, they probably deserve it," said Mrs. Peacock.

Mr. Boddy asked the guests to go to their rooms and change into the bowling outfits.

Several minutes later . . .

Several minutes later, the properly attired guests joined Mr. Boddy in the Hall.

After allowing each of them to select a ball and bowl a few practice frames, he divided the guests into two teams.

"Mrs. Strike, Greenie, and Hot Dog, you're team number one. Red, Peewee, and Birdie, you're team number two," said Mr. Boddy. "Since this is our first time, we'll only bowl two frames and we won't give extra points for strikes and spares. Team number one, you're up!"

Mrs. Strike led off.

Her first ball knocked down four pins. Her second turn knocked down three more.

Red followed. She threw a perfect strike on her first ball.

"Ten points," said Mr. Boddy. "Excellent."

Greenie was next. Unfortunately, his first ball veered sharply to the left and fell into the wooden trough alongside the lane.

"Gutter ball!" taunted the other team. "No score!"

"Quiet," replied Greenie. "Watch this one."

His second ball veered sharply to the right, plopped into the gutter, and rattled its way past the undisturbed pins.

Hanging his head in shame, Greenie trudged back to his team and wept into a bowling towel.

"No points for your team," said Mr. Boddy.

Peewee approached the lane. "I'll have you know that I was champion of my youth league," he boasted.

Peewee reared back, but released the ball too late. It knocked down a single pin. His second throw resulted in the same outcome.

"Champion?" sneered a member of the other team. "It must have been a one-player league."

Birdie was next.

Showing surprisingly good form, her first ball knocked down all but the two corner pins.

"You're left with the dreaded seven-ten split," said Mr. Boddy, sadly shaking his head. "It's almost impossible to pick up."

Birdie gave it her best. But her ball sailed midway between the two standing pins.

"If this were football, that would be a field goal for three points," said Mr. Boddy. "But, unfortunately for your team, this isn't football."

"Wait a second," complained Colonel Mustard. "She went out of turn!"

"You're right," said Mr. Boddy, consulting the scoring sheet. "Therefore, I'll take five pins away from Birdie's team."

"You can't do that!" protested Birdie. "It's rude!"

"Well, you can give up your chance at winning twenty thousand dollars," said Mr. Boddy.

Birdie and her team reluctantly accepted the pin reduction.

Mr. Boddy turned to team number one and added, "Two of you take turns now. Then it shall be team number two's turn again."

A confident Hot Dog threw the ball so hard that it shook the entire room. But his turn resulted in only six total pins.

Mrs. Strike followed. "All of my years mopping floors have built up my arm strength," she said.

Sure enough, she knocked down six pins with the first ball, and four with the second.

"That's a spare," said Mr. Boddy.

"Can you spare a spare?" asked Peewee.

It was the other team's turn. Letting go a mighty shout with each toss, Red matched Mrs. Strike's pin count. "Lifting heavy jewelry can build muscles, too," she taunted team number one.

Secretly, Peewee poured some oil into the finger holes of Greenie's ball.

Strangely, though, this prank *improved* Greenie's previous pin total by four pins.

27

To get even, Greenie tripped Peewee when Mr. Boddy updated the scoring sheet.

Unable to stop himself, Peewee hurled his bowling ball. It soared across the Hall and dropped in the middle of the pins like a bomb.

"Strike!" shouted a happy teammate.

"I planned it that way," joked Peewee.

Peewee's team began a wild victory dance — until Mr. Boddy interrupted. "I'm taking away three points for the display of bad sportsmanship." Glaring at Birdie and Red, he added, "And bad sportswomanship, too."

Laughing at the other team's misfortune, Hot Dog picked up the wrong, and smaller, ball. "Watch this," he boasted, approaching the lane.

He threw the ball with all his strength, but his fingers remained caught in it. Hot Dog and the ball skidded down the alley and slammed into the pins, knocking them down.

"Strike!" shouted Mrs. Strike.

"That's not fair!" protested the other team.

"It was a mighty demonstration of determination, but I must agree," said Mr. Boddy. He subtracted three pins from Hot Dog's effort.

Birdie checked the scoring sheet.

"A win for my team is in the bag," she said confidently, wiping her ball clean with a towel.

She approached the line and released the ball ever so carefully. At first, it was heading right for the pins, but a lack of speed caused the ball to drift further and further from the lane. Somehow it jumped over the gutter and ended up striking the grandfather clock.

"Hickory, dickory dock," mocked Mrs. Strike.

" 'In the bag', huh?" taunted Greenie. "In the clock is more like it."

"Take points away for bad behavior," Red told Mr. Boddy.

"Make them forfeit!" shouted Peewee.

"Enough! I'm taking five pins away from each team," said Mr. Boddy. After doing so, he turned to Birdie.

"Throw the last ball, please."

She did, knocking down three measly pins.

WHICH TEAM WON?

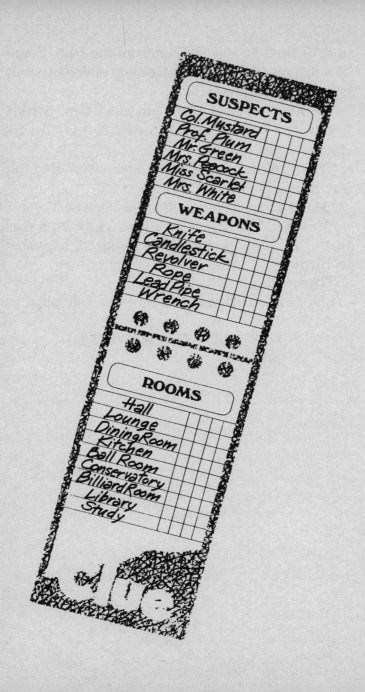

SOLUTION

TEAM NUMBER TWO: MRS. PEACOCK, PROFESSOR PLUM, and MISS SCARLET

The final score was team number two with 30 points, and team number one with 29 points.

Whatever bad feelings remained between the teams soon evaporated when Mr. Boddy brought in the traditional bowlers' meal of pizza, pretzels, cold onion rings, undercooked hot dogs, soggy french fries, stale popcorn, and pitcher after pitcher of flat soda pop. Everyone had such a good time that they forgot about the prize money. By the time they remembered, it was too late — Mr. Boddy had spent the money on gold-plated bowling balls.

4.
The Money Tree

MR. BODDY GATHERED HIS GUESTS IN the Conservatory. "I have something unusual to show you," he said. "Have you ever seen a tree quite like this one?" he asked.

"Never," replied Colonel Mustard. "What kind of tree is it?"

"Well, its bark is strange," said Professor Plum. "Maybe it's a dogwood."

"Or an elder," said Mr. Green.

"No, it's too young to be an elder," said Colonel Mustard.

"Then maybe it's a palm," said Mr. Green.

"Or perhaps a plum tree?" suggested Mrs. Peacock.

"It's not a plum," said Professor Plum. "After all, I should know."

"Whatever it is, it looks like it could use some serious sprucing up," said Miss Scarlet. "Have you considered consulting a tree surgeon?"

"Don't be a sap," said Mrs. Peacock. "There's a likely explanation why this tree looks so unusual."

"Mr. Boddy, can we get to the root of this?" asked an impatient Colonel Mustard.

"How do you explain the unusual color of the leaves?" asked Mr. Green. "They're either gold or silver."

"They look like someone sprayed them with metallic paint," said Miss Scarlet.

"It must be a fake tree," said Mrs. Peacock. "Merely decoration."

"I assure you all that the tree is very much alive," said Mr. Boddy. "This is a money tree."

The guests thought he was joking — until Mrs. White attempted to water the plant.

"Don't do that!" warned Mr. Boddy.

But it was too late.

"You almost ruined my money tree!" he stormed at his maid.

"Your what?" asked Mrs. White. "I thought you were kidding."

Mr. Boddy pulled down one of the leaves and passed it around, to the guests' amazement.

"It's a solid piece of gold," said Colonel Mustard.

"It *is* a money tree," said Professor Plum. "Well, it made a monkey out of me."

"The only one in the world," said Mr. Boddy proudly.

"Money *can* grow on trees," said Miss Scarlet. She checked her purse for the Knife.

Professor Plum touched the Wrench in his

pocket, wishing he could use it to knock some more leaves off the tree.

"But look at this mess," Mr. Boddy said, pointing to the water on the floor.

"I'll go to the Kitchen and get a mop," said Mrs. White. She was happy for an excuse to leave because she had left the Candlestick in the Kitchen.

"If you ever need anyone to prune the tree, I'm available," said Professor Plum.

"The Plum pruning. Think about it," joked Miss Scarlet.

"I'll be the only one tending this tree," said Mr. Boddy.

"And I'm tending toward stealing it," mumbled Mr. Green, checking the Lead Pipe in his jacket pocket.

Suddenly, one of the pure silver leaves dropped to the floor.

"Oh, no," said Mr. Boddy. "It's losing its leaves."

"Autumn was always my favorite season," said Mrs. Peacock.

As the guests hurried to help — help themselves, that is, to the silver and gold leaves — a male guest sneaked behind Mr. Boddy and attacked him with the Rope.

He swept the gold and silver leaves into his pocket and fled to the Lounge and then to the Hall.

There, he was attacked by the guest with the

Candlestick, who took the leaves into the Study.

The guest was about to hide the leaves when she was attacked by the guest with the Wrench.

The guest with the Wrench took the leaves into the Dining Room, but couldn't remember what to do next. "Oh, yes," he told himself, "I mustn't *leave* these where they can be seen."

He was about to hide the gold and silver leaves between the table leaves when he was attacked by the guest with the Knife.

The guest with the Knife grabbed the leaves and ran through the Kitchen and Ball Room, fearful that someone was in pursuit.

The guest with the Lead Pipe *was* in pursuit, and the two guests met in the Library.

"Leave me the leaves and you can leave," said the second guest.

"These leaves are very poplar — I mean, popular," noted the first guest, trying to run away.

The two guests struggled, and the gold and silver leaves exchanged hands.

The guest with the valuable leaves went into the remaining room, and there was attacked by a guest with the only remaining weapon.

WHO RAKED IN THE LEAVES?

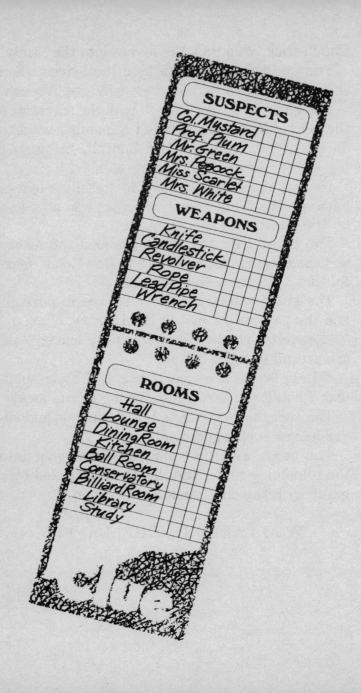

SOLUTION

MRS. PEACOCK with the REVOLVER in the BILLIARD ROOM

By process of elimination, Mrs. Peacock is the only guest not previously associated with a weapon or a room.

Unfortunately for Mrs. Peacock, Mr. Boddy forgot to tell his guests that the leaves were actually chocolates, covered in cheap foil. Foiled by this news, Mrs. Peacock consoled herself by eating several branches worth of candy.

5.
Window Pain

ONE MORNING MR. BODDY SURPRISED his guests by insisting that they help him with a difficult chore — washing the windows in the mansion.

"I don't do windows," sniffed Miss Scarlet.

"How rude to even ask!" stated Mrs. Peacock, raising her raised eyebrows even higher.

"I'm allergic to glass," said Mr. Green, moving away from the Dining Room windows.

"Working that hard would break me," said Colonel Mustard, covering a big yawn.

"Clearly I just can't see myself washing windows," said Professor Plum.

"Why don't we do something else?" suggested Mrs. White. "After all, I spend part of my day cleaning windows."

"Think of it as a window of opportunity," said Mr. Boddy, not a man to give in to pressure.

"Opportunity for what?" asked Professor Plum.

"For helping out poor Mrs. White, who works so hard on behalf of all of us," explained Mr. Boddy.

"That's her job," said Miss Scarlet. "And it's our job to have a good time and enjoy ourselves."

"So much for gratitude," sighed Mrs. White.

"True," said Mr. Boddy. "But in this case I must insist that all of you lend a helping hand."

"They only have helpless hands," said Mrs. White, glaring at her boss's lazy guests. "And I wait on them hand and foot!"

"I put my foot down at that remark," said Colonel Mustard, reaching for the Revolver.

"Stop!" commanded Mr. Boddy. "Here's the bottom line. Anyone who doesn't help will not be invited back. Anyone who does help will be rewarded."

"Rewarded?" asked Mrs. Peacock.

"Yes," said Mr. Boddy, "richly rewarded."

"How?" asked Mr. Green, leaning forward eagerly.

"With gold coins," said Mr. Boddy. "In fact, we'll divide up into teams. The team that washes the most windows will receive a pile of gold coins."

"I love to do windows!" said Miss Scarlet.

"I guess it wouldn't break me," admitted Colonel Mustard.

"Let's get cracking!" said Professor Plum.

Suddenly he realized what he had said, and he added, "Not the windows, of course."

"This is more like it," said Mr. Boddy. "We'll have three teams of two people. Each team will have a man and a woman."

"Like Adam and Eve," said Mr. Green.

"I didn't know that Adam and Eve washed windows," said a puzzled Professor Plum.

"Team number one will be Mrs. Peacock and the man whose last name starts with the same initial as hers," said Mr. Boddy.

"What about me?" asked Miss Scarlet.

"You'll be part of team number two, along with the man whose name is also a color," said Mr. Boddy.

The remaining people glared at each other.

"I'm not working with her," said the male guest.

"The feeling's mutual, only more so," shot back the female.

"So you're not competing for the gold coins?" asked Mr. Boddy.

Not wishing to be left out, the remaining two agreed to become team number three.

"Now, meet me in the Hall," said Mr. Boddy, "and we'll begin."

Several minutes later . . .

Several minutes later, the guests met in the Hall, where Mr. Boddy handed each team a bucket, a set of sponges, and window-cleaning tools.

"Let's begin!" he told them.

And they all set off.

40

"Come this way," Mrs. Peacock said to her team member. "We'll go to the Conservatory."

"Why there?"

"It has the most windows in the mansion," she replied.

Sure enough, the two washed ten windows in that room.

Team number two remained in the Hall, where they quickly cleaned two large windows.

Team number three headed back to the Dining Room, where they washed five windows. But they overlooked one because it was partially covered by a large potted palm.

Then Professor Plum had to make an unexpected stop to find his glasses and his team stopped momentarily.

Mrs. White led her team to the Kitchen, where she was very familiar with all the windows — even the hidden ones in the pantry. Her team washed a total of seven windows there.

Moving on to the Study, team number two washed six windows there.

Then team number one rushed to the Library, only to realize that the room had just one *huge* window! It took the team twenty minutes and much grumbling.

Team number two moved to the Ball Room and triumphantly washed five windows.

Team number one washed one more in the Lounge.

41

Team number three washed one more in the remaining room.

The teams reported back to Mr. Boddy. He tallied their totals, then made a surprising announcement: "Two teams are tied!"

"But there are no more windows to wash," said Miss Scarlet.

Mr. Boddy checked his addition. "According to my tally, there is one window still to be washed."

Everyone frantically rushed around the mansion until one of the teams discovered the window hidden behind the potted palm.

"Hurrah!" shouted Colonel Mustard as he put all of his energy into washing the final window.

WHO WON?

HOW MANY WINDOWS DID EACH TEAM WASH?

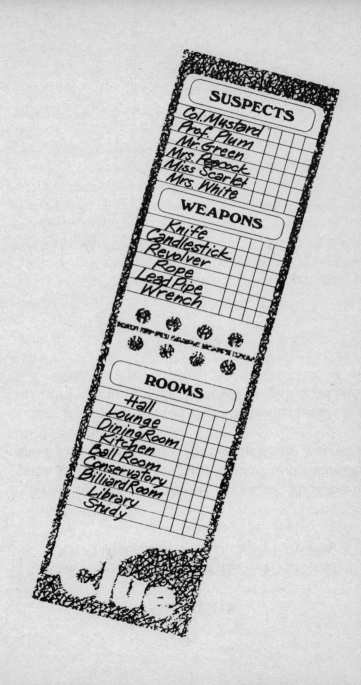

SOLUTION

Team number three: MRS. WHITE and
COLONEL MUSTARD, with fourteen
windows.

Team number two (Miss Scarlet and Mr. Green)
came in second with thirteen, and team number
one (Mrs. Peacock and Professor Plum) lost with
only twelve.

Mr. Boddy suggested that the teams tackle the
upstairs windows next. Instead, they tackled him.

6.
By George

GLANCING INTO THE STUDY, MR. Boddy saw Professor Plum about to lick a postage stamp and glue it to an envelope.

"Don't use that stamp!" shouted Mr. Boddy, rushing in.

"Why not?" asked Professor Plum. "It's a perfectly good stamp."

"I'll show you a perfectly good stamp," said Mr. Boddy. He pounded his foot on the floor. "There. Now hand over that stamp."

Professor Plum sheepishly did as he was ordered.

"I'm sorry," he said. "I only wanted to send a card to my dear aunt Martha."

"Didn't you look at the stamp closely?" asked Mr. Boddy.

"Not really," admitted Professor Plum. "Should I have?"

"It's rare and valuable," said Mr. Boddy.

Professor Plum began to laugh, convinced that Mr. Boddy was joking.

But Mr. Boddy was not joking. "Look at the

face on the stamp," he instructed Professor Plum.

"It's George Washington," said Professor Plum. "Washington, D.C. — Daddy of our Country. Nothing strange about that."

"Look closer," said Mr. Boddy.

Professor Plum did.

"Is his white wig crooked?" he asked.

"No," said Mr. Boddy.

"Are his eyes crossed?" asked the professor.

"Of course not," said Mr. Boddy.

"I read somewhere that Washington had wooden teeth," said Professor Plum. "Did he forget them for this portrait?"

"That's not it, either," said Mr. Boddy. "But you're looking at the right place, which is Washington's mouth."

"He doesn't have a piece of spinach stuck between his teeth?" asked Professor Plum.

"No, no, no," said an exasperated Mr. Boddy.

Professor Plum shrugged his shoulders. "I give up," he said.

"Look at the expression on his face."

At last, Professor Plum saw what Mr. Boddy was talking about. "Why, George is smiling!" he noted. "That *is* unusual."

"It was a printer's error," said Mr. Boddy. "Only a few full sheets of stamps were printed before the post office caught the mistake and stopped the press run. The mistake was quickly corrected, but not before a few hundred smiling

Georges found their way into circulation. Such a stamp is instantly valuable to the discerning collector, like myself. Each of the misprinted stamps is worth fifteen thousand dollars."

"Fifteen thousand dollars to mail a letter?" said a shocked Professor Plum. "Talk about inflation!"

Mrs. White entered. "Look what someone left in the Billiard Room," she said, holding up the Candlestick.

"Look at Mr. Boddy's rare stamp," said Professor Plum.

Mrs. White stared at the stamp. "George Washington is smiling," she observed. "I never saw a smiling George before."

"Exactly," said Mr. Boddy.

The whites of Mrs. White's eyes widened. "That must be a very valuable oddity," she said.

"Oddity?" asked a hurt Professor Plum. "Are you talking about me?"

"No," she assured him, "I'm talking about George."

Overhearing the conversation, Mrs. Peacock entered. "Someone put this dirty Knife back in the Dining Room drawer," she said, waving the weapon. "It's the height of bad manners — and laziness — to try and pass off dirty eating utensils as clean." She glared at Mrs. White.

"Don't look at me," Mrs. White said. "Here, trade weapons with me and I'll make sure it's wiped clean when I return to the Kitchen."

47

The guests traded weapons.

"Well, well, what's going on?" asked Mrs. Peacock.

"Our host is showing us a stamp worth fifteen thousand dollars," said Professor Plum.

"Is this the truth?" asked Mrs. Peacock.

"I cannot tell a lie," said Mr. Boddy. "This George Washington stamp is worth exactly that."

Mr. Green entered, carrying the Wrench.

"Where are you going with that?" asked Mrs. White.

"To the Lounge, where Colonel Mustard wrenched his back dueling a sword-wielding robot."

"Are you going to wrench Colonel Mustard's Wrench?" asked a puzzled Professor Plum.

"Actually, I'm going to adjust the robot to save the colonel further injury," said Mr. Green. "What's so interesting here?"

"Mr. Boddy was showing us a very valuable stamp," said Mrs. Peacock.

Intrigued, Mr. Green took a look. "By George, Washington is smiling," he said.

Knowing an oddity when he saw one, Mr. Green started scheming to steal the stamp later.

"Well," he added, heading for the door, "I told the colonel I'd be right back, so please excuse me."

As he left, he bumped into Miss Scarlet.

"Hey, watch that Wrench!" she said.

"Watch that Rope," he responded. "You could have strangled me."

A smile came to Miss Scarlet's lips. "What a wonderful idea. Maybe next time."

She moved into the room and learned about the smiling George stamp.

"I'll bet a collector would pay a great deal of money for that," she said.

"Mr. Boddy said it's worth — " started Mrs. White.

"I just about had to crawl in here on all fours," interrupted Colonel Mustard. He was holding his lower back and was in obvious pain. "But my dear friend Mr. Green reported that Mr. Boddy has a stamp of enormous value."

"It's true. But, Colonel, you're in no condition to do anything but rest," advised Mr. Boddy.

"Rest? I'm first in war, first in peace, first in the hearts of my countrymen!" stormed Colonel Mustard. He got himself so worked up that he threw his back out again.

"Here," said Mr. Boddy, "let me help you to your room."

Mr. Boddy started to help Colonel Mustard toward the door.

However, when Mr. Boddy's back was turned, one of the remaining guests stole the valuable stamp and hid it in the palm of her hand.

The thief soon left the room and went into the Hall, heading, in fact, for the front door.

"I need to get to town before the coin and stamp store closes," she told herself.

But as she reached for the front doorknob, she was attacked by the guest with the Candlestick, who stole the stamp.

The guest with the Candlestick went into the Conservatory, planning to hide the stamp there.

But in that room she was surprised by the guest with the Knife.

"I'll take George off your hands," the guest with the Knife said, fleeing into the Library.

Meanwhile, in the Hall, Colonel Mustard attacked Mr. Boddy with the Lead Pipe. He planned to steal the stamp for himself.

In the Library, the guest with the stamp was surprised by the guest with the Wrench and lost smiling George.

The new thief raced into the Kitchen. There was a cherry pie cooling on the counter. "Hmmm, perhaps I should hide Washington in there," murmured the thief. "No, too obvious. . . ."

The thief next tried the Dining Room and then the Lounge and then the Billiard Room, but could not find a good hiding place. The thief then decided to attempt leaving the mansion undetected.

The guest mused, "I'll go to the stables, mount Vernon, my horse, ride into town, and sell George."

But in the only room no one had been in all day,

the thief was hit over the head with the Lead Pipe and fell to the ground.

The attacker stole the stamp.

"I cannot tell a lie. It looks like I've licked the competition for this stamp," he said. "This Washington will earn me a huge stack of one-dollar bills."

He was about to hide the stamp when another guest entered and ordered, "Give me the father of our country."

The guest with the stamp asked, "How much is it worth to you?"

"Fifteen thousand dollars," the second guest said. "Now hand it over, or I'll be forced to use my weapon."

Having no alternative, the first guest handed over the stamp to him.

WHO WAS THE LAST PERSON TO STEAL
THE STAMP? IN WHAT ROOM?
AND WITH WHAT WEAPON?

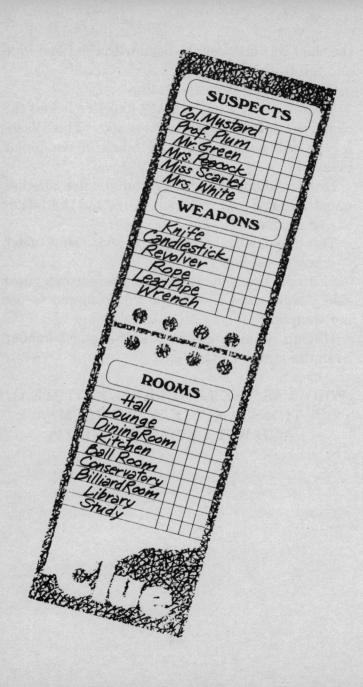

SOLUTION

PROFESSOR PLUM with the REVOLVER in the BALL ROOM

The solution can be found by process of elimination. Also, in the last word of the story the thief is identified as male. Further, Professor Plum is the only male who knows the exact worth of the stamp.

Professor Plum smiled as he looked closely at the smiling George stamp in his hand. Then his smile turned to a frown. Earlier, Mr. Boddy had secretly switched stamps while he was talking to the guests. Instead of smiling George, Professor Plum now held a stamp with a little, round, yellow smiley face and the words "Have a nice day" underneath. It was worth less than one cent.

7.
To Top It Off

LATE ONE AFTERNOON, MR. BODDY strolled into the kitchen. He found Mrs. White still cleaning up after the lavish lunch she had prepared and served to the guests earlier.

"Mrs. White," said Mr. Boddy, "may I have a word with you?"

"A word is all I have time for," said Mrs. White. Standing at the sink, she was up to her elbows in suds. She pulled out a pan, now scrubbed clean, and rinsed it under the faucet. Then she set it on the drying rack.

"I need to talk to you about dinner," said Mr. Boddy.

"I was afraid of that," said Mrs. White. She took a towel, dried her hands, turned, and faced her employer. She seemed on the verge of tears.

"Mrs. White, what is the matter?" asked Mr. Boddy.

"I regret to inform you that I haven't had a chance yet to go to the market," she reported. "I'm planning a four-course supper from soup to nuts. You and your guests will not be disappointed. It's just that I'm a bit behind schedule, given your guests' particular culinary wishes."

"I see," said Mr. Boddy.

"Take lunch," she continued. "I had planned a nice meat stew for everyone. Something simple yet filling. Then Miss Scarlet decided she'd prefer a watercress and cucumber sandwich. Colonel Mustard refused to eat any stew containing meat he himself had not hunted. Mr. Green complained that the carrots and potatoes were too soft and insisted that I serve him the turkey leftovers from last night. Mrs. Peacock found the stew much too spicy and accused me of making rude food. Professor Plum — "

"I understand," interrupted Mr. Boddy. "Which is why I'm here."

"You mean you're firing me?" asked a stunned Mrs. White.

"On the contrary," said Mr. Boddy. "I found the stew absolutely delicious. You are a wonderful cook, Mrs. White."

"Then what's the problem?" asked a skeptical Mrs. White.

Mr. Boddy chuckled. "There's no problem," he assured her. "You work much too hard."

"Tell me something I don't know," sighed Mrs. White.

"As a reward for your hard work, I'm giving you the night off from cooking," said Mr. Boddy.

Tears welled up in Mrs. White's eyes. "You

are?" she whispered. "That's so nice. But what are the guests going to do for dinner?"

"I've already taken care of it," said Mr. Boddy. "I've ordered four pizzas to be delivered to the mansion. Once they arrive, I hope you will join me and the other guests in the Dining Room."

"Thank you, kind sir," said Mrs. White.

Several minutes later . . .

Several minutes later, the front doorbell rang and Mr. Boddy answered it. A pizza delivery person wearing a silly uniform and an enormous oven mitt handed over four pizza boxes. Mr. Boddy paid for the pizza and tipped the delivery person handsomely.

Mr. Boddy carried the four pizza boxes into the Dining Room, where the guests were already seated around the table.

Being a careful host, Mr. Boddy had already polled his guests to determine what kinds of pizzas would best satisfy their individual whims.

"I believe that everyone will be most pleased with these pizza pies," said Mr. Boddy, putting the boxes down in the center of the Dining Room table. "There are four pies. Each contains eight pieces, so there should be plenty for everyone."

He opened the first box. It contained a plain cheese pizza with no additional toppings. "This is what you, Mrs. Peacock, requested," said Mr. Boddy.

"Precisely," she said with a grin. "Toppings of any sort other than cheese are an abomination to the word *pizza*."

"That's an awfully big pie," noted Mr. Green. "If Mrs. Peacock can't finish it all by herself, I'd be happy to have a piece."

A few of the other guests also offered to eat cheese.

Mr. Boddy opened the other boxes. "Miss Scarlet," he continued, "I took into account your preference for strictly vegetarian toppings."

"How gracious of you," she said with a smile.

"Colonel Mustard, I remembered that you eat only meat toppings," said Mr. Boddy.

"A man's man's man's pizza," said Colonel Mustard, pounding the table with his fist.

"Professor Plum, you wanted mushrooms or pepperoni, right?" asked Mr. Boddy.

"I think so," said Professor Plum, trying to remember. "In any case, puprooms and musheronis will more than satisfy my appetite."

"Don't you mean mushrooms and pepperoni?" asked Mrs. White.

"Isn't that what I said?" asked a bewildered Professor Plum.

Mrs. White said she would eat anything.

"I hope you remembered that I wanted green pepper or any meat," said Mr. Green.

Mr. Boddy assured him that he had.

On closer inspection, the guests discovered that one pie was half green pepper and half black olive, a second pie was half mushroom and half sausage, a third pie was strictly pepperoni, and the fourth was plain cheese.

A few of the guests were hesitant to eat.

"Is there a problem?" asked Mr. Boddy.

"Some pies are half one topping and half another," said Colonel Mustard.

"So?" asked Mr. Boddy.

"Look how that mushroom has crept near that nice hunk of sausage," Colonel Mustard said, pointing to the second pie.

"So?" asked Miss Scarlet.

"I won't eat any meat-topped piece from a pizza that also has half vegetable-topped pieces," he said. "It's icky. And cowardly. Have you ever heard of a brave hunter stalking a wild broccoli?"

"Fine," said Miss Scarlet. "And I won't take any vegetable-topped pieces from a pie that is half meat-topped!"

"Are we going to argue or eat?" asked a hungry Mr. Green.

Mr. Green took one piece of green pepper pizza and one of pepperoni.

"I'm hungry, too," said Mrs. Peacock, taking three pieces of the pie with no special toppings.

"Wait for me," said Miss Scarlet. She took two pieces, one with black olives and the other topped with a different vegetable.

"Look," said Mr. Boddy, pointing to a pizza, "none of you have touched this pie."

To make their host feel better, Professor Plum took a piece from the vegetarian half and Mr. Green took one from the meat half.

"I'm so happy to have a night off from cooking that, like I said, I'll eat anything," said Mrs. White. "So here goes."

Mrs. White took a piece of each of the toppings and one of cheese.

"You're going to eat three-quarters of a pie all by yourself?" asked an astonished Mr. Boddy.

"Watch," said Mrs. White, biting into a piece topped with mushrooms.

"I'd better load up before all the slices I prefer are gone," said Colonel Mustard.

By himself, Colonel Mustard quickly devoured half of the all-meat pie.

Not to be outdone, Miss Scarlet ate the remaining black olive pieces.

"Professor, you're falling behind," said Mrs. White, starting on her piece topped with pepperoni.

To catch up, Professor Plum took a piece of each kind of pizza he preferred.

"How is it?" asked Mr. Boddy.

"Delicious," said Colonel Mustard, his cheeks bulging with food.

Mrs. Peacock daintily wiped the corners of her mouth with a napkin. "It's rude to speak with your mouth full," she said. Turning to Mr. Boddy, she added, "Although the quality of the cuisine is not up to Mrs. White's high standards, I find the pizza very much to my liking."

"I'm so glad," said Mr. Boddy.

All this time, Mr. Green was eyeing the pizza that Colonel Mustard wouldn't touch. While the other guests commented on the delicate blending of cheeses, sauce, and spicing, Mr. Green gobbled up two meat-topped pieces from that pie.

Colonel Mustard, having finished what was on his plate, was still hungry. "I'll help you, Mrs. Peacock," he said. And he quickly helped himself to two pieces of the pizza she preferred.

Mrs. White took a similar piece and another of the vegetarian topping favored by Professor Plum.

"It's almost all done," noted Mr. Boddy.

Finally, Mr. Green finished the last vegetarian slice as well as the last slice of the all-meat pie.

This left only one slice of Mrs. Peacock's pie, which Miss Scarlet ate.

Mr. Boddy surveyed the scene. There were four empty pizza boxes and six very full guests.

"Congratulations," he said. "You've eaten everything that I ordered. Well done!"

60

The guests, holding their stomachs, their cheeks bulging, could barely manage a nod.

"Now," said Mr. Boddy, "who's ready for dessert?"

WHO ATE THE MOST PIECES?

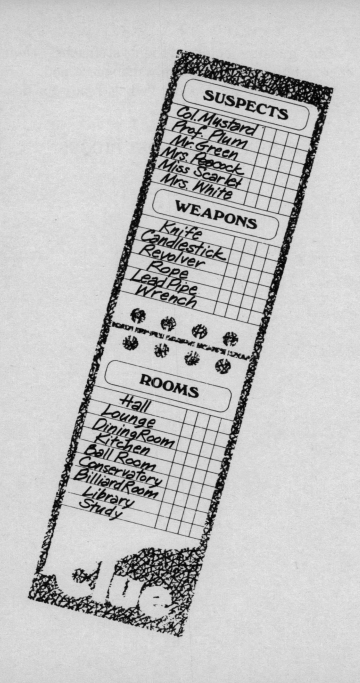

SOLUTION

MRS. WHITE

Mrs. White ate eight pieces: two cheese, one green pepper, one black olive, two mushroom, one sausage, and one pepperoni.

For dessert, all the guests preferred an antacid followed by a long nap.

8.
Holy Toledo

MR. BODDY ASKED HIS GUESTS TO
come to the Hall.

There, he drew their attention to one of the
suits of armor on display.

"We've seen your splendid display of medieval
armor before," noted Colonel Mustard.

"Do you notice anything different about this
one?" Mr. Boddy asked, pointing to one near the
grandfather clock.

The guests studied the armor intently.

"You raised the arm a little?" asked Mrs. White.

"No," said Mr. Boddy.

"You polished the armor to a new and improved
shine?" asked Mr. Green.

"It's not that," said Mr. Boddy.

"Mr. Boddy is a wonderful boss but, believe me,
he never polishes anything," said Mrs. White.
"Except the night he polished off three bowls of
chunky double-fudge chocolate ice cream."

"Well, this won't be a good night unless Mr.
Boddy tells us about his good knight and does so

this very instant," warned Colonel Mustard. He waved the Lead Pipe to back up his threat.

"This particular knight is holding a new sword," said Mr. Boddy.

"It doesn't look new," said Mrs. Peacock. "It looks like it could use a polish."

"Will you stop," asked Mrs. White, "before I polish you off with this?" She held up the Wrench.

"If you want to polish," said Mr. Boddy, "the Candlestick is looking a little tarnished." He handed it to his maid in exchange for her weapon.

"If anything is tarnished, it's your reputation," Miss Scarlet told him. "How dare you take up our valuable time with some worthless old sword."

"Miss Scarlet is right — for once in her life," added Colonel Mustard. "I'm so furious that I'm about to challenge you to a duel!"

"In truth, the sword *is* old," explained Mr. Boddy. "It's only new to my collection. It belonged to the king of Spain four hundred years ago."

"The king of Spain?" echoed Mr. Green. "Kings generally have an enormous amount of money. It comes with the job."

"Look at the jewels and precious stones on its golden handle," said Mrs. Peacock, taking a closer look at the sword.

"Oh, it's decorated to the hilt," said Mr. Boddy.

"Didn't the king of Spain reign mainly on the plain?" asked Professor Plum.

Ignoring him, Mr. Boddy said, "The sword was made by the finest craftsmen in Toledo."

"Toledo? Ohio?" asked Mrs. Peacock. "I think not!"

"Toledo, Spain," said Mr. Boddy. "It's a city south of Madrid, famous for its high-quality steel artifacts."

"Holy Toledo," whispered Mr. Green, reaching into his pocket for the Knife. "I'd like to steal that steel."

"Me, too," said Colonel Mustard. "I will be bored without the sword."

"I'd be on the cutting edge if I owned that blade," muttered Miss Scarlet.

It was getting late. "Time to retire," Mr. Boddy told his guests. "We'll leave the knight in charge of the Hall."

"Good knight — I mean, night," said Professor Plum.

Several hours later . . .

Several hours later, a male guest with the Rope entered the Hall.

Not wishing to leave his fingerprints on the suit of armor, he carefully looped the Rope around the sword and then yanked it free.

"Since I can't afford this sword," he said, "I must hide it under the chessboard."

He took the sword into the Study, thinking he

had last seen the chessboard there. But the chessboard was not in the room.

He next tried the Library. The chessboard was there on top of a draped table.

But before the thief could hide the sword under the drape, he was attacked by a guest with the Revolver.

"Swords may be crude and weapons rude," the guest said, "but stealing this one's pretty shrewd."

She took the sword into the Dining Room. Her plan was to toss it out of a window and retrieve it later.

But the plan was ruined when she saw a male guest already in the Dining Room.

Before she could retrace her steps and try another room, the male guest spotted her and jumped to his feet. Quickly she tried to hide the sword behind her back.

"What's that you're hiding?" he asked.

"Nothing," she lied.

"Come on, I can see it sticking out," he said.

"Oh, it's a back-scratcher," she said.

"Don't treat me like an imbecile," he warned. "I know it's Mr. Boddy's valuable sword."

"You're right," she said, whipping the sword in front of her.

She began to advance on the male guest.

To her surprise, though, he shouted, *"En garde!"* and lunged forward with the Lead Pipe.

"Sir, I'll have you know that I took fencing lessons as a girl," she said.

"Then you're a worthy opponent," he said confidently.

The two guests began to parry and thrust. First, the female guest had the advantage, then the male guest. Back and forth, blade and pipe crashing against each other, the guests struggled.

She jumped on the Dining Room table and he followed. Down the length of the table they fought. He jumped off first and dashed out of the room. She gave chase, only to have him surprise her outside the door.

But she proved herself an expert swordswoman and forced him back, back, back into the Ball Room.

There, the classic battle was joined by a third guest with no weapon. She waited for the exact moment, then pounced on the first female guest and came away with Mr. Boddy's prized sword.

The second female guest dashed through the Conservatory and into the Billiard Room, thinking she could hide the sword among the cue sticks.

But there she was attacked by the guest with the Knife.

He took the sword and went into the remaining room, where he was hit over the head by the remaining guest and passed out.

WHO'S HOARDING THE SWORD?

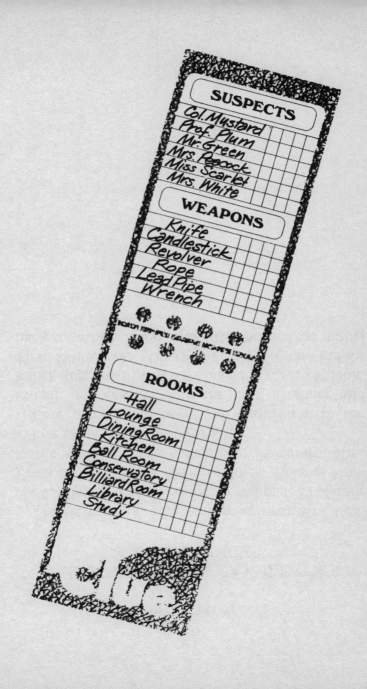

SOLUTION

MRS. WHITE with the CANDLESTICK in the LOUNGE

The reference to rudeness gives away Mrs. Peacock. Miss Scarlet never had a weapon. Professor Plum had the Rope, since we know Colonel Mustard's and Mr. Green's weapons. Therefore, Mrs. White must have the sword.

Later, trying to leave the mansion with the sword, she crashed into the suit of armor and knocked it down, waking Mr. Boddy. At last look, Mrs. White was still trying to piece the knight back together. There was little peace that night!

9.
Musical Chairs

AFTER A VERY LARGE AND SATISFYING meal in the Dining Room, Mr. Boddy invited his guests into the Conservatory.

"If it's all the same, I'd like to go upstairs and rest," said Mrs. Peacock.

"And I was planning to watch some paint dry," said Mr. Green, stifling a yawn with his hand.

"I'd rather go into the Library and read the dictionary," said Miss Scarlet.

"And, of course, there are dishes for me to do in the Kitchen," sighed Mrs. White.

But Mr. Boddy insisted. Once in the Conservatory, he told the guests, "I have a new CD recording of Beethoven's Fifth Symphony I want you all to hear."

"I'm fairly tired myself," said Colonel Mustard, "after a long day of dueling. Perhaps we can listen to one half of the Fifth."

"Did Beethoven write a Symphony Number Two-and-a-Half?" asked Professor Plum.

"Or I have a suggestion," said Mr. Green. "We

can forget Ludwig and listen to something short. Like *The Flight of the Bumblebee*."

"Oh, honey, that's a good idea," said Miss Scarlet.

"Sorry, but I can't listen to bee music," said Colonel Mustard. "It makes me break out in hives."

"I could handle a little Handel," said Mrs. Peacock, "but I'll pass on the Beethoven."

"Or I'd back up Bach," added Mrs. White.

"I like that composer whose name sounds like a type of ice cream," said Professor Plum.

"Ice cream?" asked Mrs. White.

"You know, Fran Sherbet," said Professor Plum.

Mrs. Peacock rolled her eyes. "You mean Franz Schubert."

"I once got my hair cut while listening to Samuel Barber," said Mr. Green.

"It's Beethoven, or you can pack your bags," insisted Mr. Boddy.

The guests reluctantly agreed to go along with their host's plan.

"But where are we going to sit?" asked an indignant Mrs. Peacock, looking at an assortment of mismatched chairs.

There was one plush upholstered chair, a rocker, a love seat that could seat two people, a hardbacked wooden chair, and one folding chair.

"Do we get a free stuffed animal with every chair purchased?" joked Mr. Green.

"I'm sorry about the strange assortment of furniture," said Mr. Boddy. "You see, I'm in the middle of redecorating."

Mrs. Peacock quickly claimed the plush chair.

Mr. Green claimed the rocker.

Colonel Mustard and Mrs. White shared the love seat.

Professor Plum grabbed the wooden chair.

And because she didn't act fast enough, Miss Scarlet was forced to take the folding chair.

With the guests seated, Mr. Boddy placed the CD in the player.

Soon Beethoven's famous opening was heard through the Conservatory's expensive sound system.

But there was a problem with the seating arrangement.

Mr. Boddy stopped the CD. "What's going on?" he asked.

Mrs. White had fallen asleep against Colonel Mustard and he didn't like it. "Get this woman off of me," he demanded.

"What did you expect, sitting in a love seat?" asked Mr. Green, who exchanged places with Colonel Mustard.

Mr. Boddy started the music over from the beginning again.

But less than a minute later, another guest threatened to leave. "This folding chair is most uncomfortable," complained Miss Scarlet.

Professor Plum graciously changed places with her.

Mr. Boddy started the famous symphony for the third time.

Then Mrs. Peacock fell asleep in her chair.

Mr. Boddy snapped off the CD player. "Let me settle this," he said.

Mr. Boddy decided to put the two sleepy guests together. The displaced guest took Mrs. Peacock's previous place.

Mr. Boddy started the music for the fourth time.

Colonel Mustard listened intently and soon was moving back and forth to the music.

"Must you?" complained Miss Scarlet.

"Must I what?" asked Colonel Mustard.

"Your chair is making too much noise," she said. "This isn't rock and roll."

Mr. Boddy snapped off the music. "You're acting like a bunch of children," he told his guests.

Apologizing for the group, Colonel Mustard changed places with Miss Scarlet.

Mr. Boddy started the music again, for the fifth time.

"Maybe this is why they call it Beethoven's Fifth," suggested Professor Plum.

A moment later, Mr. Boddy changed his mind.

"There's no reason for anyone to sleep through such glorious music."

He had Mrs. Peacock change places with Professor Plum, and Mrs. White change places with Mr. Green. He started the music once more.

But soon, Mrs. White, in the most comfortable chair, was snoring away again.

"Make her take my chair," said Colonel Mustard. "It'll help keep her awake."

Mr. Boddy agreed, and the guests changed places.

At last, the seating arrangement seemed to be working — until Miss Scarlet demanded another change.

"No, this is the end to this game of musical chairs," insisted Mr. Boddy.

With that, he ejected the CD and headed for the door.

WHO IS SEATED WHERE?

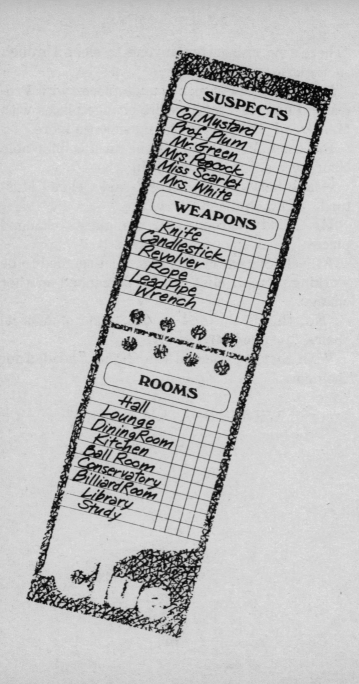

SOLUTION

COLONEL MUSTARD is in the plush upholstered chair, MISS SCARLET has the rocker, PROFESSOR PLUM and MR. GREEN share the love seat, MRS. WHITE is in the hardback wooden chair, and MRS. PEACOCK occupies the folding chair.

As Mr. Boddy left, his guests gave him a standing ovation. This annoyed him so much that the next time Mr. Boddy wanted his guests to stay put, he equipped the furniture with locking seat belts — and kept all the keys.

10.
The Dangerous Diamond

"**W**HERE'S MRS. PEACOCK?" MR. BODDY asked the other guests in the Hall.

"She's taking the *secret* secret passage from the Kitchen and meeting us in the Study," said Mrs. White.

Mr. Boddy nodded. "Well, we can start without her. Have you heard of Fort Knox?" he asked his guests as he led them toward the Study.

"Yes," said Mr. Green. "That's where the government guards its gold bullion."

"Bouillon?" asked Professor Plum. "The government spends our tax money guarding soup? No wonder some people stay home on election day."

"Not bouillon," said Mr. Green. "Bullion. Bars of solid gold."

"Come with me," Mr. Boddy said, "and I'll show you my personal Fort Knox."

He had the guests stop just outside the Study door.

"Watch your feet as you enter," warned Mr.

Boddy. "I've installed trip wires at every entrance and exit."

The guests carefully stepped over the wire just inside the door.

"You're taking no chances," observed Mrs. White.

"You'll see why in a moment," said Mr. Boddy.

In the room was a glass case. Displayed inside was an enormous, flawless diamond.

"How many carats is that?" asked Mr. Green.

"It's in excess of three hundred carats," Mr. Boddy assured his guests.

"I hope that's the Hope Diamond," said Miss Scarlet.

"Actually, it's called the Dangerous Diamond."

"Dangerous?" Miss Scarlet batted her eyelashes. "But why?"

"The previous owners were always in danger of having it stolen. So it was dangerous to own, you see." Mr. Boddy smiled. "Of course I won't have that problem. Not with my state-of-the-art security system. I'll have to think of a new name for the diamond."

Suddenly, Mrs. Peacock entered from the *secret* secret passageway and nearly fell over the trip wire guarding it.

"How rude!" she shouted, fighting to regain her balance.

Without warning, alarms and strobe lights started going off.

Mrs. White covered her ears.

Colonel Mustard covered his mouth.

Mr. Green covered his eyes.

Professor Plum's knees began to shake. "Whatever I did, I'm sorry!" he shouted.

Finally, Mr. Boddy moved to a control unit on the wall and disarmed the alarms and strobe lights.

"My word!" said Mrs. Peacock. "I nearly did a swan dive! What was that horrible wire?"

"I'll explain in a moment," said Mr. Boddy. "Please step forward and take a gander at my diamond."

"It's called the Dangerous Diamond," said Mr. Green. "It's so valuable, it's dangerous to own."

"Well, not anymore," said Mr. Boddy.

"It looks like it weighs a ton," said Mrs. White.

"How rude to talk about my weight!" snapped Mrs. Peacock, who was still upset about losing her balance.

"I was talking about the diamond," explained Mrs. White.

"It doesn't weigh a ton," laughed Mr. Boddy. "But more than a few pounds, I assure you."

"Have you had it for a long time?" asked Miss Scarlet.

"For years," replied Mr. Boddy. "It was locked away in a safe-deposit box."

"And you never told me?" asked Miss Scarlet, pouting.

"I always wanted it on display," explained Mr. Boddy, "but I waited until I had the best security system money could buy."

"You mean it's impossible to steal it?" asked a disappointed Colonel Mustard.

Mr. Boddy proudly nodded.

"Maybe you should call this room Fort Not instead of Fort Knox," suggested Mrs. White, "since the diamond cannot be stolen."

"What exactly have you installed?" asked Mr. Green, hoping to steal the diamond himself.

"Besides the trip wires, I've installed a latch on the display case that is activated by heat," said Mr. Boddy.

"Tricky, tricky," said Mr. Green, making certain he had the Lead Pipe in his pocket.

"The diamond itself rests on a platform that is protected by a counterweight system," added Mr. Boddy.

"I've heard of counterfeit, but counterweight?" asked Professor Plum.

"Meaning the diamond can't be removed without the system's detecting the sudden absence of weight," said Mr. Boddy.

Mr. Boddy directed the guests' attention toward the ceiling.

"Overhead," he continued, "is a twenty-four-hour surveillance camera."

"What's that heavy mechanism on the back of the door?" asked Professor Plum.

"A bolt and lock system that I operate with this," said Mr. Boddy, pulling out a small remote control. "Don't think of stealing the remote. I'm the only person who knows the secret code to punch in to operate it. Please notice that there's a similar device on the back of the door leading to the *secret* secret passageway."

"Looks like you've thought of everything," said a depressed Miss Scarlet, slipping the Knife back into her purse. "I, for one, promise you that I won't be a threat. I'm going into the Dining Room to enjoy a nutritious snack. If I can't satisfy my wish for the diamond, at least I can satisfy my tummy."

"And I need to tend to some Dueling Club business in the Ball Room," said Colonel Mustard.

"Mind your feet on the way out," advised Mr. Boddy. "You don't want to trip the trip wire like poor Mrs. Peacock did."

Miss Scarlet and Colonel Mustard left at the same time, carefully stepping over the trip wire when they reached the door.

"And I'm retiring to the Conservatory," said Mrs. Peacock. "I need to finish a book report for *The Journal of Modern Manners*."

"Well, I have some beds to make upstairs," said Mrs. White. She carefully stepped over the trip wire on her way out.

"And I need to check the latest business news

on TV in the Lounge," said Mr. Green. He exited, as well.

"Congratulations on your security apparatus," said Professor Plum. "I'm off to the Billiard Room to shoot a rack of balls." He took the Revolver from his pocket. "Don't worry," he said. "I wasn't going to shoot with this."

All the guests went to the rooms to which they said they were going.

After Professor Plum exited, Mr. Boddy used the remote control to bolt the door to the *secret* secret passageway.

Satisfied that the diamond was safe, he, too, left the room.

Outside the closed door, he pushed a button on the remote control and that door and the one to the *secret* secret passageway bolted themselves shut.

A little while later . . .

A little while later, a guest entered the Library and took the Wrench, which had been concealed there.

The guest hid near the door to the Billiard Room, and waited.

When another guest left the Billiard Room, he was attacked by the hiding guest and lost his weapon to the assailant.

The successful thief moved to the Hall and waited for the guest in the Lounge to leave that room.

When the guest left the Lounge, he was hit over the head with the Wrench and was knocked out. He lost his weapon in the process.

A different guest heard the commotion and, grabbing the Candlestick, came running from the Ball Room.

But the guest with the Candlestick fell victim to a surprise attack and lost his weapon to the guest still lurking in the Hall.

The marauding guest next ventured to the Dining Room and disarmed the guest there and took her weapon.

"I have everything I need to steal the diamond except one last weapon," the guest said. Then she remembered that the remaining guest was in a room writing a report.

The guest went to that room and demanded the writer's weapon.

"To every great writer, the pen is mightier than the sword," the report-writing guest proclaimed.

"Since you don't have a sword, I'll settle for your weapon," the first guest said.

After a brief struggle, the first guest came away with the report writer's weapon.

Dashing upstairs, the guest opened a window and used a weapon to rappel down the outside wall of the mansion, stopping outside the Study window.

There, the guest pushed open the window, but did not enter until first slicing apart the trip wire near the floor.

Having successfully entered the room, the guest immediately shot out the surveillance camera overhead.

"So far, so good," the guest said.

The guest approached the diamond in the display case.

Then the guest took a weapon which holds a heat source and warmed the display case latch until it snapped open.

Next, holding a heavier weapon, the guest snatched the diamond and simultaneously left the weapon in its place. Doing this, the guest outsmarted the counterweight system.

With the diamond in hand, the guest avoided a second trip wire near an exit that was not the door to the room.

There, the guest used the final weapon to loosen the bolts on the exit and escape with the diamond.

Unfortunately, the guest encountered Mr. Boddy in the next room.

"So, it looks like my security sytem isn't so wonderful," he observed.

"Not to someone clever like me," the thief said.

"Give me back the diamond and we'll forget the whole thing," said Mr. Boddy.

"You seem to be forgetting one thing," said the thief.

"And what is that?" asked Mr. Boddy.

"I have all of the weapons," said the thief.

"Oops," said Mr. Boddy. "The Dangerous Diamond is still dangerous after all."

The guest quickly arranged the weapons in the same order they were used to steal the diamond and murdered Mr. Boddy with the third one.

WHO MURDERED MR. BODDY?
WITH WHAT WEAPON?
AND IN WHAT ROOM?

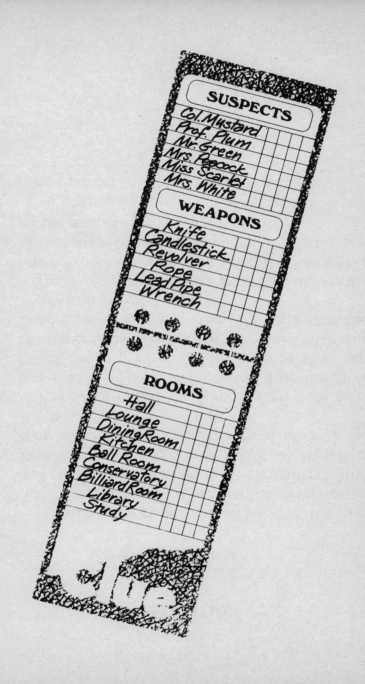

SOLUTION

MRS. WHITE with the REVOLVER in the KITCHEN

Since the male guests were eliminated, the murderer must be female. We know that Miss Scarlet had the Knife in the Dining Room and that Mrs. Peacock was writing a book report, so Mrs. Peacock had the Rope. This left Mrs. White with the Wrench.

Mrs. White used the Rope (taken from Mrs. Peacock) to rappel from the second floor, the Knife to cut the trip wire, the Revolver to shoot out the camera, the Candlestick to heat the latch, the Lead Pipe to take the diamond's place, and the Wrench to loosen the bolts.

The *secret* secret passage from the study is the other exit that was bolted shut. It leads to the kitchen, as noted at the beginning of the story and on the map of the house.